ME as a baBY + GranDMA ANN

AunT JeN ↳

AunT GRACE ↰

SaIIy

SIMON & SCHUSTER BOOKS FOR YOUNG READERS
An imprint of Simon & Schuster Children's Publishing Division. 1230 Avenue of the Americas, New York, New York 10020. Text copyright © 2000 by Karla Kuskin. Illustrations copyright © 2000 by Dyanna Wolcott. All rights reserved including the right of reproduction in whole or in part in any form. SIMON & SCHUSTER BOOKS FOR YOUNG READERS is a trademark of Simon & Schuster. Book design by Lily Malcom. The text of this book is set in Bembo. The illustrations are rendered in gouache and watercolor. Manufactured in China. 12 14 16 18 20 19 17 15 13 11
Library of Congress Cataloging-in-Publication Data. Kuskin, Karla. I am me / by Karla Kuskin ; illustrated by Dyanna Wolcott.—1st ed. p. cm. Summary: After being told how she resembles other members of her family, a young girl states positively and absolutely that she is "NO ONE ELSE BUT ME." ISBN 978-0-689-81473-0 [1. Identity—Fiction. 2. Family life—Fiction.] I. Wolcott, Dyanna, ill. II. Title. PZ7.K965Iam 2000 [E]—dc21 98-7911 CIP AC
0811 SCP

I Am Me

WITHDRAWN

by Karla Kuskin

illustrated by Dyanna Wolcott

SIMON & SCHUSTER BOOKS FOR YOUNG READERS

Everybody says I have my mother's eyes, her pointed chin.

My coloring is like my dad's,

I'm also like him, being thin.

My hands are Mom's.

My feet are Dad's,
except my funny little toe,
which is a lot more like Aunt Jen's.

My voice is like hers too,

quite low.

"Those eyebrows," says my father
with a happy stare,
"I'd know those eyebrows anywhere.
Your grandma Ann had eyebrows just like those,

And Mother's ears.

BIKES

The color of your hair
is really Sal's but Sally's tends to curl
and yours gets lighter in the sun,
like Mother's did when she was still a girl."

"Your smile," says Mom,
"reminds me of my sister Grace,
the way it's crooked
and the way it lights your face."

I clear my throat to speak
standing up straight,
as straight as any tree.
"While everything you say is true,"
I say,
"it's also true
without a doubt"
(I shout this out)
"that

        I

        am

positively

absolutely

altogether

NO
ONE
ELSE

BUT

ME."

This was for the new bunch:
Madeleine Margaret
and Amelia Jane,
Helen May,
Caroline,
Jake,
Carter and Mary,
Eloise and Isabelle and Jack,
Conrad and Hadley,
and Emily and Ben,
with love
—K. K.

For Sam, who will always
have her mother's heart
—D. W.